To: Gavin

A positive attitude is like
it will never misguide you!!

— [illegible] IV

1/11/2020

Printed in the United States of America First Printing, 2019

In loving memory of my grandfather, Oscar Redden Jr.

You will be forever remembered as a hometown hero, with a giant personality, a big-heart, and an inspirational leader. You always had a gift of leaving people better than the way you found them.
Your love for our family, the passion in which you served your community is a testament to your devotion to God and his people,
A true brother's keeper! Love you forever!

-Pooh

The life I have led has been full of fun.
I've soared on high winds warmed by the sun.

I've seen creatures that crawl on their bellies by night,
goats that climb mountains, and street cats that fight.

I've watched bears catching fish from the rivers and streams, and seen dogs with their owners eating ice-creams.

I've seen wolves chasing rabbits through the deep, deep snow, and watched four-hundred year old turtles walk so... so... slow

But the best that I've seen is a
well-mannered child, who treats others politely
and never acts wild.
I'll tell you the lessons I learned about life,
from bird life to wildlife to finding my wife.

The worst I've seen was a penguin thief; a criminal bird who brought others much grief. He stole stones by the dozen from friends and neighbors, building a nest by crooked endeavors.

it's him!

The loneliest beast I ever did meet was a
grumpy, old ape who wouldn't share his seat.
He lived up in the trees all his life all alone
and as he got older he started to moan.

The happiest chap I looked down upon was a horse called Oscar who ran all day long. He had three sons who all got along, and a wife called Marci who taught right from wrong.

yipeee!
whoohoo!
heehee!
come on!
watch the egg while I go shopping
xx

I know that life can be tough and cruel some days.
But do what's right, not wrong, and you'll always be praised.

Find a friend who listens, as well as speaks.
Find a job, work hard, and aim for the peak.

Albatross
chick daycare

Don't settle for anything less than the best,
and remember the homeless when you've built your nest.

Whatever you do, do it well my friend.
Do the best you can do until you reach the very end.

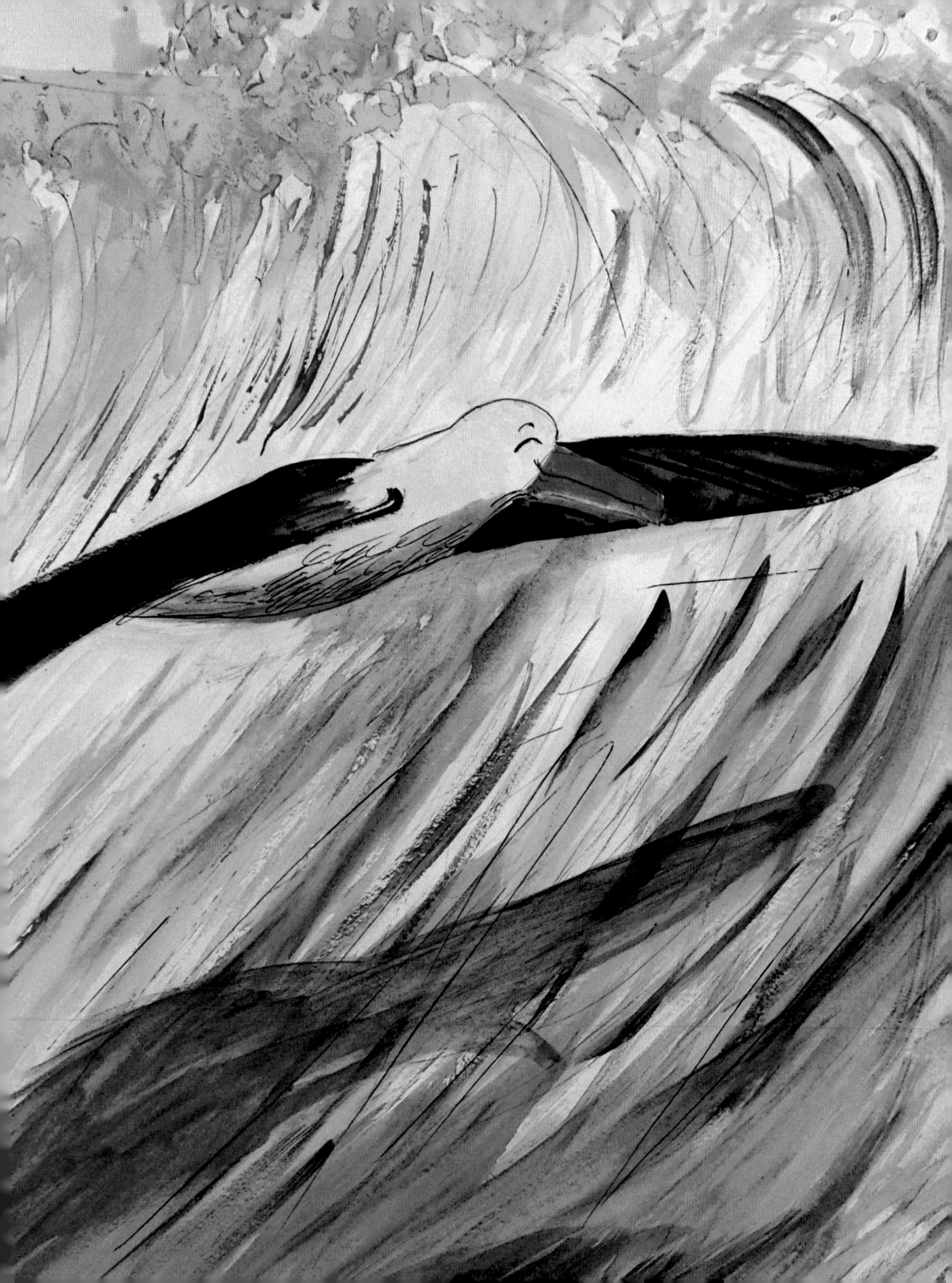

Made in the USA
Lexington, KY
13 November 2019